Africa
1 4 4 0

Kai isn't like the other girls in her Yoruba village of Ife. The boys tease her because she can run faster than they can. Even her best friend, Aisha, can't understand Kai's desire to learn how to make the beautiful terra cotta masks and bronze figures for which Yoruba craftsmen are celebrated—an art women in Ife are forbidden to learn.

When a blight on the yam crop threatens the tribe with starvation, the Oni, the ruler of Ife, chooses Kai to take a message to a distant village. But instead of the trusted Aisha, Kai must share the dangerous mission with her vain, lazy older sister Jamila. With words of wisdom and encouragement from their granny Nalo, the village headmother, the girls set out on their four day journey through the dense forest and grasslands—a journey that will change Kai's relationship with her sister forever, and bring her closer to realizing her dream.

GIRLHOOD
Journeys

Kai

GIRLHOOD Journeys

Kai

A Mission for Her Village
Africa, 1440

by Dawn C. Gill Thomas

illustrated by
Vanessa Holley

GIRLHOOD JOURNEYS COLLECTION®
ALADDIN PAPERBACKS

Grateful acknowledgement is made to Chelsea House for the use of the illustrations on pages 66 and 67 from *Yorubaland: The Flowering of Genius* by Philip Koslow; and to The National Commission for Museums and Monuments, Lagos, Nigeria for the use of the illustration on page 68.

First Aladdin Paperbacks edition October 1996
Copyright © 1996 by Girlhood Journeys, Inc.

Aladdin Paperbacks
An imprint of Simon & Schuster
Children's Publishing Division
1230 Avenue of the Americas
New York, NY 10020

Also available in a Simon & Schuster Books for Young
Readers edition.

Designed by Wendy Letven Design
The text of this book is set in Garamond.

10 9 8 7 6 5 4 3 2 1

Library of Congress Cataloging-in-Publication Data
Thomas, Dawn C.
Kai: a mission for her village—Africa 1440 / by Dawn C. Gill Thomas; illustrated
by Vanessa Holley
p. cm—(Girlhood Journeys)
"Girlhood Journeys Collection."
Summary: In fifteenth century Africa, Kai and her beautiful but lazy older sister
Jamila undertake a perilous four-day journey to another Yoruba village, seeking help
for their starving tribe after the blight of the yam crop.
ISBN 0-689-81140-3 (hardcover).—ISBN 0-689-80986-7 (pbk.)
[1. Sisters—Fiction. 2. Yoruba (African people)—Fiction. 3. Africa—Fiction.] I.
Holley, Vanessa, ill. II. Title. III. Series.
PZ7.T3664Kai 1996
[Fic]—dc20 96-15703 CIP AC

C O N T E N T S

GLOSSARY

agbo ile
A "flock of houses"
where clan
members live.

Alafin
ruler of Oyo

baba
father

bale
The elder of a Yoruba clan.

clan
A group of people
who descend from the
same ancestor.

Esho
The Alafin's elite guard of
seventy warriors.

fufu
A dish made of mashed yams.

iya
mother

lost wax method
A special method of casting
bronze sculptures used by
the Yoruba people.

Moremi
mythical Yoruba hero

nayami
yam

Oduduwa
father of the Yoruba people

Oni
The ruler of Ife and the
spiritual leader of the
Yoruba people.

ore ko-ri-ko-sun
A best friend. Literally,
"friend-not-see-not-sleep."

terra-cotta
A type of clay that becomes
very hard when heated.

tsetse fly
An insect that lives in the
West African forest and
transmits a deadly disease.

yeye ojumu
The highest ranking woman
of the elders of Ife.

yeye li oja
The woman in charge of the
market.

CHAPTER ONE

KAI'S DREAM

ilently, Kai crouched low outside the craft
huts and peered through the dense shrubs.
The sun had nearly set, and the shadows it
cast helped hide her from view. Soon the
craftsmen would be heading back to their houses
in the *agbo ile.*

Kai moved closer so she could watch the men
working. To her right, just beyond the shrubs, an
artist sat, working on a clay figure. It was coated
with a layer of beeswax, which the sculptor
molded with his hands and tools. It was the head
of an Oni, a past king of Yorubaland, and it was
beautiful. With its noble face and beaded crown,
it looked very real.

Suddenly, the artist looked around. Kai held
her breath. The art of casting sculptures was a
secret, known only to these men. If she were

caught snooping, she would surely be punished.

The artist went back to work, and Kai watched as he dipped his fingers in a pot. Carefully, he coated the wax Oni with clay until it was completely covered. When he was finished, he placed it on a mat.

Without warning, the artist stood up and called to his friends. As he did, he took a step back, nearly touching Kai.

She would have to run if they saw her. She'd climb over the village wall, into the grove, and out of sight.

The artisans weren't interested in Kai. They gathered their tools together and began to walk back to the *agbo ile*.

Kai waited a few minutes to make sure she was alone, and then crept into the courtyard where the men had been working. It was filled with beautiful statues. Some were of brass. Some were terra-cotta, waiting their turn to be fired in the oven. There were pots of beeswax everywhere, and in one corner sat a group of sculptures coated with clay. *It must take years to learn all this,* she thought.

Kai held one of the clay statues. It was a small standing figure of a man, with two small holes in

the bottom. When Kai looked in, she could see the layer of beeswax inside. Kai was puzzled. She wondered why they were using wax. It would all melt and run out through the holes when the figure was heated.

Suddenly, her thoughts cleared. *So that's how they do it!* They *want* the wax to melt. Then they pour ceramic clay or molten brass into the space where the wax had been. The sculpture, originally formed in wax, becomes now a beautiful brass or terra-cotta figure.

"So that's it," she said, this time out loud. Kai looked around to see if anyone had heard. The air was still. *I'd better leave,* she thought, *before somebody sees me.*

As she moved back into the bushes, she passed a small pit where the artists had tossed their "mistakes." It was piled high with broken pieces of clay, a few cracked terra-cotta figures, and several brass objects tarnished with black marks. It was time to go.

Kai loosened the colorful cotton wrap around her head, gathered the broken pieces into the cloth, and swung it over her shoulder like a knapsack.

When she reached the village walls, she tossed

the bundle carefully over the top onto the soft grass on the other side. She climbed over the wall and walked a short distance to the edge of the forest. At the foot of an ironwood tree Kai stopped and buried her treasures, covering them with moss. She marked the spot with a stone so she'd be able to find it again.

Kai tied the wrap around her head and raced along outside the village wall and through the front gate. As she headed up the palace walk, she admired the magnificent statues that lined the road. The sight of them always made her a little sad, since she longed to be a sculptor. In the land of Ife, only men were permitted to be trained as artisans.

"I see you, Kai."

Kai turned and saw Aisha coming up the path and slowed to allow her friend to catch up. Aisha couldn't walk very fast, dragging her left foot as she did. She walked with a limp because her foot had been damaged at birth.

"Is something wrong?" Aisha asked.

"Why would anything be wrong?"

Aisha shrugged. "You look like you need to wet your lips." Aisha was holding a calabash bowl filled with water.

"Thanks." Kai downed the water in a few quick gulps. "Friends till the winds stop blowing," she said, hugging Aisha.

"Friends till the sun stops rising," replied Aisha.

"You're my *ore ko-ri-ko-sun*."

Aisha's smile lit her face like a lantern. Only men used this name, since it meant "a friend for life" and women didn't have friends for life. When girls married, they went off to join their husbands and had to make new friends.

Kai didn't care. She called Aisha her *ore ko-ri-ko-sun,* anyway.

"Where were you?" asked Aisha. "I went to your hut, but you weren't there."

"I was out walking."

"You were spying on the craftsmen again, weren't you?"

"I saw how they cast the statues. I know the secret now," said Kai, looking around and making sure that no one overheard. "In some villages to the north, the Oni is a woman. So why can't I be an artist here?"

Aisha looked worried. "Please, Kai. Stop this. I'm afraid for you."

"I know," said Kai. "I know. But I just keep

thinking if I can make some statues on my own, the craftsmen will see that I am gifted and they will let me join them."

"Or marry you off to another village for breaking the rules of Ife. Then I would never see you again."

"Oh, don't worry so much, Aisha," said Kai, taking her hand. The two girls walked along the road, joking and laughing.

"Look there," said Aisha, pointing to a small palm grove. Kai's older sister, Jamila, lay on the grass in the shade of an oil palm, fast asleep. "Do you want me to wake her? One swift kick should do it."

Kai shrugged. If Jamila wanted to sleep, what did she care? "We should do *something,* or she'll miss the evening meal."

"I have an idea," said Aisha, walking over to the tree.

Aisha stood above Jamila and began to sing sweetly. Kai joined in, and the girls began a harvest song in near perfect harmony, singing louder and louder until Jamila stirred. After a while, the young woman stretched her arms, which were slender and elegant. She rolled her neck, which was long, graceful like a swan's.

When she stood up and finally shook the sleep from her eyes, they gleamed. Nearby villagers turned their heads, for Jamila was the most beautiful girl in Ife. "What's wrong?" yawned Jamila. "Why are you pestering me?"

"Look at her," said Aisha. "She's like one of your statues. Nice to look at, but not very useful."

"I don't *have* to be very useful," Jamila replied. "There is no prettier girl in all of Yorubaland. Everyone says so."

"That's true," said Kai. "But your beauty won't make the yams grow any faster."

"So? I will marry a wealthy man," Jamila replied.

"Well, Princess Jamila, if I were a man, I'd rather marry Kai," said Aisha. "She's got a smile that can chase the clouds away, she's smart, and she sleeps a lot less than you do."

Jamila rolled her eyes and waved her hand. "You little girls are too young to understand these things. Now, leave me in peace."

The girls laughed and continued on their way. Jamila was only thirteen, and very silly for her age, but she often tried to act like a mature woman of the village.

The palace walk led to the Ife market

square, a large clearing across from the Oni's royal residence. It was surrounded by large trees that provided shade for the women who sat on mats selling their wares. There were melons, peppers, and gourds. Pottery and utensils were on display.

The market was getting noisier and more crowded every minute, as people were arriving from all over the land of Ife. It was the week's end, so the market was more like a festival. Farmers came carrying calabashes and corn, weavers and dyers bought bolts of cloth, and herbalists hawked their roots and flower medicines.

Kai made her way through the crowds, Aisha following close behind.

"Where are we going?" asked Aisha.

"To see my granny Nalo."

"But she'll be busy," said Aisha.

"She may be *Yeye Ojumu,* Head Mother of the village, but she's never too busy to see me, her favorite granddaughter," boasted Kai.

"Kai. *Kai!*"

Someone was shouting. Kai turned and saw her brother, Bahati, shepherd staff in hand. He gently kicked his flock out of the way. "Where is Granny?" Kai asked.

"She is with *Yeye li oja,*" said Bahati. "You

should hurry to her hut. She has asked for you by name."

"Oh." If she was with the Mother of the Market, it meant something was up.

"You go on ahead," said Aisha. "I'll meet you there."

"Okay. See you," replied Kai, breaking into a run. Some of the men watched her, for although Kai was short for her age, she was very fast on her feet. She was only ten, but she had already won kola nuts by defeating several older boys in foot races. As she ran, Kai darted in and out, around mats piled high with fruits and vegetables. Several shepherd boys yelled at her as she leaped over some baby goats, frightening the herd and scattering the animals.

When Kai arrived at the Mother of the Market's hut, she wasn't even breathing hard. She tiptoed inside, trying not to make a sound.

"I see you, Kai."

She winced. No matter how softly she walked, Granny always heard her approach. "And I see you, Jamila," laughed Granny.

Kai whirled around to see her sister standing behind her. A pack of young boys were outside the hut, staring in at Jamila and giggling like clowns.

"If you want to stay and watch my granddaughter, I will put you to work," chuckled Granny, raising her voice so the boys could hear her. "*Lo, lo,*" she called out, commanding them to leave.

The boys jumped when they heard the voice of the Head Mother. One of the boys shouted back, "We are not here to look at Jamila, but to race against Kai. Are you sure she's not your grand*son?*"

"Be gone," said Granny angrily, and they all scattered. "Never mind them," she said to Kai. "They do not tease those whom they do not like."

"I *am* your grandson, and I see you, Granny Nalo." It was another voice outside the hut.

"I see you, Bahati," said Granny, "but I did not send for you. When I am in need of mischief, then I will call."

The other boys laughed. "I will be the man of the house someday," said Bahati, storming off in a huff.

Granny sighed. "Bahati, always trying to run before he has learned to walk."

The Head Mother wore a brightly colored robe made of two large rectangular pieces of cloth, tie-dyed in patterns of red, purple, green, and blue. Her hair, now mostly gray, was braided by other women in the village. Her eyes were closed, but you could see them move under the lids, as if she were still able to see. Now and then she opened her eyes, and you could see that they were milky white where they once had been brown.

"I see you, Head Mother," said Aisha, giving Jamila a little shove as she entered the hut.

"I see you, sweet Aisha." Granny smiled and reached out to Kai, holding her granddaughter's face in her hands, which were warm like the rays of the sun. "Hmm," she said, running her fingers over Kai's head, "your wrap is covered with clay dust."

Granny held Kai's hands in hers and stroked them. "Wax under your fingernails, no? It feels like molding wax. But how could that be?"

Uh, oh, thought Kai. But before she could answer, Granny turned to Jamila, moving those delicate fingers across Kai's sister's face. They fluttered like a bird across her soft cheeks and smooth skin and gently over her eyelashes.

Granny laughed. "Sleeping again? I suppose poor Kai did your share of the weaving today."

"How does she know these things?" whispered Aisha. "She's been blind for many years."

"No one is like Granny Nalo," Kai whispered back. "Everyone says so. She's never needed eyes to see the truth about things. She can feel it."

Kai turned to Granny. "I don't mind doing Jamila's work," she said. "I love the weaving. I—"

"Hush." Granny held her hand up, and Kai fell silent. No one spoke. Granny reached into the folds of her robe and produced a small *nayami.*

"Yams! The harvest must be early!" said Jamila. "Now you can make me a *fufu* and vegetable soup."

Granny Nalo said nothing. She just rolled the yam in her palms. Her face grew dark.

Kai scooped a yam from the bowl at Granny's feet. It was so soft that her fingers left dents in its hairy brown skin, which was covered with a pale green film. "What's wrong with them?" she asked.

"They are blighted," said Granny.

"What does that mean?" asked Aisha.

"Now and then Nature plays a cruel trick and takes away the yams that we need for our food. They wither and rot before we can harvest them. The farmers have told the Mother of the Market that all the yams in Ife are blighted."

"Are we going to starve?" asked Jamila fearfully.

"I think you will not be taking many long

naps," laughed Granny. "It's hard to sleep on an empty stomach, no? Except for me." Then Granny Nalo put her head down and fell fast asleep herself, the blighted yam still in her hand.

The girls looked at the Mother of the Market, who had been listening all the time. Her eyes were wet with tears. "Pray that we don't go hungry," she said. ❖

THE ONI'S MISSION

Kai moved to the throbbing rhythm of the talking drums. The musicians pressed on the drums' leather cords, changing the tone and pitch of the drumbeats so they sounded as if they were "talking" in praise of the great chiefs. As she danced, she arched her back and arms gracefully, imitating the animals and the spirits of the forest. The drumming grew faster and louder, but she kept with the beats. *I don't have Jamila's beauty,* she thought, *but I can dance as well as she can.*

The music ended, and Kai sat down, rubbing her feet by the fire. They were tingling. Suddenly, they felt ticklish and then a little damp.

A little damp! Kai sat up on her sleep mat, awakening from her dream. A small goat was licking her feet. "Bahati," she shouted, "get this goat out of here!"

"Uh-oh," said Bahati, rolling out of bed and shaking his fist at the goat. He stood up and gave it a shove. "Come on, get out."

"Bahati."

"Too late," laughed Kai as her father entered their sleeping compound.

"What is this smelly goat doing in your corner?" he asked his son.

Bahati prodded the goat with his staff, but it refused to budge.

"I am waiting for an answer," said Father.

"What an odor," complained Jamila.

Bahati looked around. Granny and Mother were awake. Mother's eyes wandered from the goat to poor Bahati and then back to the goat. Granny Nalo covered her face, hoping that her grandson couldn't see her laugh.

"My son, you bear the markings of a man on your face," said Father, pointing to the small, decorative scars worn by men of Yorubaland. "Now, behave like one."

"The goat is in the house, *Baba,* because I

trained him to come wake me if he doesn't see me by grazing time."

Baba looked at Bahati sternly for a few seconds, but then roared with laughter. "Nonsense! You forgot to pen the goats last night, and they got loose."

Bahati knew he was saved as soon as he heard the sound of the talking drums announcing the coming festival. Suddenly the goat wasn't important, as everyone went about the business of preparing for the festival.

Kai and Jamila rose quickly and readied themselves. They rubbed their bodies and hair with palm kernel oil and powdered their faces with camwood.

"How can we celebrate the yam harvest when there are no yams?" whispered Kai.

"I'm sure I don't know. But help me with this," Jamila replied, producing a small shell filled with a soft gray paste.

Kai sighed. "Oh, Jamila, you're too young to wear eye color."

"Please," whined Jamila, sounding more like three than thirteen.

"All right." Carefully, Kai ran a thin coat of galena around her sister's beautiful eyes.

"You look like a
princess," said Kai,
trying not to show her
envy.

"I'm not finished,"
said Jamila as she
rubbed her skin with
dyes made from roots
and berries.

Next, Kai and Jamila draped
themselves in their finest cloths, tying them
around their waists and over their shoulders.

"I see you, *Iya*," said Kai as their mother
appeared in the doorway. She looked at them, but
didn't say a single word. She didn't have to. "We
are almost ready, Iya."

"The rest of the house is waiting, and so are
the clan elders."

The family headed out to the front of the
compound, where the rest of the clan was
gathered behind the eldest man, who was called
the *Bale,* the "father of the house."

Aisha greeted Kai and her sister as they
stepped from their corner into the road. "Are you
getting married today, Jamila?" she asked.

"Of course not. Why?"

"You look like you are dressed for a wedding," replied Aisha, laughing. Kai laughed, too.

As they went along, the group grew larger. Other clans from different parts of the town were arriving, as were clans from smaller farm villages outside the walls.

The Bales were dressed in flowing ceremonial robes. The village workers, potters, weavers, and other artisans followed, their crafts decorated with feathers and beads. Their robes bore symbols showing the work they did.

The procession came to a stop in front in the palace courtyard, facing the Oni's beautiful palace with its fine veranda. The seven town chiefs, each surrounded by his Bale and a guard of clan warriors, took their positions. As they awaited the arrival of the Oni's personal servant of announcements, the drummers beat out messages praising the king and wishing him long life.

Suddenly, the drumming grew louder, and a procession emerged from the Oni's palace and took its place on the veranda. The tribal chiefs, honored warriors, and the wise men of Ife, all in colorful ceremonial robes, stood facing the doorway to the palace. Kai beamed with pride when she saw Granny Nalo among them.

The Bales were summoned into the palace. After them, the clan elders were called.

Again, the drumbeat changed, and the Oni, wearing his colorful beaded crown, walked slowly out onto the porch. His crown had a fringe, which covered his entire face like a beaded curtain. Some of the fringes were decorated with little birds. There were beautiful beads on his robes, sandals, and seat cushions as well, and he held a whisk made of ram's hair.

One of the king's servants stepped forward. "The Oni of Ife, supreme ruler and spiritual leader of the Yoruba people, wishes to speak with the child Kai and the maid Jamila, grandchildren and direct descendants of Yeye Ojumu, Nalo."

Kai played with one of her braids. Jamila knew it meant that her sister was afraid, even though she would never say so. The two girls looked at their parents and their Bale. They didn't smile or frown. Instead, they just nodded in the direction of the Oni.

Slowly, the girls made their way toward the Oni's palace. The crowd parted, making a path for them. It took only a few minutes to walk the short distance, but to Kai, it seemed like hours.

Jamila walked beside her, and although she looked radiant, none of the men or boys giggled or called out to her as they usually did. They knew that if the Oni wished to speak to Kai and Jamila, the girls had to be very important indeed.

"Halt," one of the guards commanded.

"Me?" asked Kai.

"No," he replied, pointing to someone standing behind her. "Who are you?"

"I am Aisha, friend and companion of Kai," said Aisha, trying to sound very official.

"Well, friend and companion of Kai," said the guard, "you will have to remain outside."

Aisha frowned, but the guard was kind and let her stay where she was, just a few feet from the Oni himself.

An official of the king stepped forward to meet them, and the Oni stood up and went inside to his throne room. As he passed by Granny Nalo, he gestured to her with his whisk, and she rose and followed him inside.

"Enter," said the official. Kai began to tremble. She looked at Jamila, who was about to cry. Only the highest-ranking elders had ever seen the throne room of the Oni. *What could he want with us?* she wondered. *It can't be good.*

The Oni was sitting on his throne chair, which was decorated with brass carvings. His servants were all around him, cooling him with fans made of marabou feathers. His feet rested on a beautiful beaded cushion. Beside it, at his feet, Granny Nalo sat on her haunches.

"Welcome, my young ones," said the Oni in a kindly voice. He began to wave his whisk playfully. Kai couldn't see his face through the beads, but he seemed to be in a good mood.

"I see you, Oni of Ife, the supreme ruler of the Yoruba," whispered Granny, poking the girls with her walking staff.

"I see you, Oni of Ife, the supreme ruler of the Yoruba," repeated the girls. The Oni laughed, his belly bouncing under his beaded robe.

Abruptly, the laughing stopped, and the Oni leaned forward. "You know of the misfortune that has befallen our people?"

"Yes, my Oni," said Kai. "The yams are blighted."

"What is your mother's trade?" he asked.

"She is a weaver and dye maker. The best in all the kingdom of Ife."

"Good." The Oni leaned back on his throne.

The precious stones on his headdress glistened as he tossed his head from side to side. "Now, I have a mission for you." The Oni reached behind him. "Take this," he said, handing Kai a beautiful hardwood staff with a delicate brass head on the top.

Kai's eyes grew wide. "That's a fine casting. Someday I will make them, too."

For a few moments, the king said nothing. Kai looked at Granny Nalo, who seemed to be holding her breath. Then they heard the Oni laugh once more.

"This staff bears the head of Oduduwa, father of the Yoruba, and the symbol of the Oni," he said. "Whoever sees it will know you are my messengers."

It seemed as if Kai had forgotten where she was. She stared at the sculpture and opened her mouth to speak. Jamila gave her a kick, but Kai kept on going. "I know how to cast such figures."

The Oni leaned forward once more. "My child, you are a bold one. Now, I can banish you to the forest for your disrespect, or send you

there on a mission to help save our village from
starvation. What shall the great Oni do?"

"May I take my friend Aisha?"

Granny shot Kai an angry look and shook her
head.

"You may take anyone you like. As long as it
is your sister, Jamila," said the Oni.

"We will go wherever you wish, Oni," Jamila
said.

Granny Nalo looked up when she heard
Jamila's voice. It was the first time the young
woman had spoken in the Oni's presence.

"Good. You will take the forest road to the
north. In less than four days' time you will reach
a large village surrounded by two walls. This
village is Oyo. In Oyo, you will see the Alafin,
who rules there, and you will tell him of our
misfortune, and that we are in need of food. You
will also tell him that next spring, we will repay
him with goats, sheep, calabash, yams, and many
fine crafts. The Alafin will send men with grain,
and you will return with them."

Kai grew more nervous and played with her
braid. She wished Aisha were going instead of her
fancy sister, who would probably complain all the
way to Oyo. Even with her lame foot, Aisha had

learned to swim and worked hard helping her mother. She played all the games as well as the other girls. Aisha rarely complained and she never gave up.

"But, Oni, we have never been outside of Ife," said Jamila. "Why have you chosen us? We know nothing of the forest and the land beyond."

The Oni did not answer, but he turned his head toward Granny Nalo.

"You will find out when you reach Oyo," said Granny. She beckoned to the servants, who came to her side and helped her to her feet. She reached into a pouch and took out two leather thongs, each with a small brass figure attached. "These two figures were once attached by a chain," said Granny. "I now give one to each of you."  She placed one around each girl's neck. "Show them to the Alafin when he greets you. He will know you by these figures."

"Why can't I come with you?" sobbed Aisha.

Kai frowned. Aisha was very sensitive to even the slightest insult, and Kai hated to hurt her feelings. "The Oni said—"

"I know what the Oni said."

A cool breeze drifted through, gently shaking the leaves of the baobab tree. The long, hanging fruit swayed in the wind. This giant tree was the friends' favorite spot, shady, cool, and quiet. This was where they came to talk about things.

"Then you know why you can't come," said Kai.

"Did you ask him if I could come along?"

"Yes," she said. "But the Oni insisted I take Jamila instead."

"Granny Nalo doesn't think I'm strong enough. I can walk for miles without resting. You know that."

"I know that, and so does Granny. She is very fond of you."

"You said we'd never be apart."

"We won't. It is just a few days' walk to Oyo. I'll be there and back in less than two weeks."

Aisha began to weep. "Oh, Kai, I'm afraid. What will I do if something happens to you?"

The two girls hugged tightly. Kai's sadness turned to anger. She knew she was Aisha's only true friend, because the other children teased her. *Why were they so cruel?*

"I will be fine," said Kai. "After all, I have Jamila to protect me."

"Now you know why I'm so afraid," said Aisha.❖

CHAPTER THREE

THE JOURNEY BEGINS

Kai and Jamila stood just outside the main gate of Ife. Kai wanted to cling to the gates, fall to her knees, and beg the Oni to send someone else on this mission. Jamila, who looked even more frightened, watched her sister's every move. *This is no time to show fear,* thought Kai.

Just ahead was a twisting dirt path leading into the forestland, worn smooth by the footsteps of Yoruba hunters. The path was bathed in sunlight for a few yards, but the girls could see it soon turned dark in the shade of the tall, thick trees as it disappeared into a maze of deep, dense bush.

On their heads, the girls carried bowls made of calabash gourds and covered with cloth. Inside were the things they would need for the journey.

There were woven mats for sleeping, and wooden spoons and cups. There were roasted melon seeds, yam *fufu,* and toasted peanuts. Each girl carried a goatskin filled with water, and a long brass knife given to her by the Bale for cutting through dense bush.

Kai turned for one last look at her village. Mother, Father, Granny Nalo, and other clan members stood in the gate, singing with the beat of the talking drums that seemed to speak their names. Children sat on the walls or peered over them. Others stood and watched along the walls. It seemed as if the entire village had come to see them off, except for the Oni, who never left his palace grounds.

"Coming through," said Bahati, making his way through the crowd to where Granny Nalo sat. "How could the Oni have chosen my sisters for so important a mission?" he demanded to know. "Am I invisible?"

"You question the Oni's judgment?"

"What do you think of this? What does Granny Nalo, yeye ojumu, think?"

Granny took a breath and summoned all her patience. "Bahati, this journey is not without danger. With the village short of food, all men will be needed to hunt for game, and to defend us from attack from our enemies. Grown women have other duties. Sending your sisters is a wise choice."

Bahati stomped his feet and hit the ground with his staff, which made the bells at the top ring. "It is not a mission for young girls."

Aisha stood a short distance away. Suddenly, she began to run toward the sisters. "Kai," she called out. "Wait!"

Kai turned around. "I will return in one week," she said.

"Good luck," said Aisha. "I will watch over you. If you feel alone, just think of me."

"I will. You are my *ore ko-ri-ko-sun*."

Granny Nalo slowly stepped forward, clapping her hands to draw the villagers close around her. She placed her hands on the faces of her granddaughters, caressing them with her gnarled fingers. "Toss your troubles under the baobab tree when you pass by. Don't worry. They'll still be there when you get back," she said, roaring with laughter. "I will see you soon, my beloved Kai and my precious Jamila."

"Let's go," said Kai, beginning to walk. Kai heard Jamila begin to whimper. "How bad can it be?" said Kai. "Granny Nalo is still laughing." The drumming grew louder, but the girls didn't look back.

They could still hear the sounds of the village when they reached the edge of the forest, but they could no longer see it. The air was cooler, and the ground was moist. The chattering of monkeys and the shrill cries of birds called from every tree.

For the first few miles the sisters did not speak to each other. Each was lost in private thoughts. Kai missed her friends already, and she longed to dig up and examine her buried treasure of art.

"Can't you walk faster?" With her bouncing stride, Kai was far ahead of Jamila.

"My pace is just fine," said Jamila.

"So *you* say," said Kai. "I'm going to get to Oyo in less than four days. If you fall behind, too bad."

"If *you* fall behind, *too bad,*" said Jamila, imitating her sister.

Kai began walking even faster.

"What was that?" asked Jamila. A high-pitched shriek shot through the forest, echoing through the trees.

"Don't you know a hyena when you hear it?" Kai responded scornfully.

"Is that what it was? A hyena? I thought perhaps it was one of your friends."

Kai just shook her head. Even Bahati would have been a better companion.

As they walked further, the forest overwhelmed them. The ferns were very tall, towering over them like huge arms. The flowers, although beautiful and fragrant, were unfamiliar. Strange birdcalls and animal noises surrounded them. Every now and then, their nostrils were filled with the odor of a dead animal or decaying fruit.

"Kai," asked Jamila in her friendliest voice, "was that really a hyena we heard?"

"I think so. But it sounded very far off. Granny said that this road is well-traveled, and the scent of humans keeps most animals away," replied Kai. "All we have to do is watch under our feet for creepy-crawlers that might be lurking."

Although they could barely see the sun, the forest grew hot and damp in the midday heat. As Kai walked, she kicked over a rock and several lizards slithered out from underneath.

Kai shuddered. Sweat began to pour down her face. She was getting tired. "Hey, Jamila, why don't you sing something? It'll make you feel better."

Jamila didn't answer.

"Jamila?" called Kai.

"Shhhhh."

Kai turned to see Jamila stopped in her tracks, staring straight up at something. She held a rock in her hand.

"What is it?" Kai whispered.

"Look at that bird. It's got green feathers. I want a few for my hair."

"And you are going to kill that poor bird to get them?"

"Can you think of a better way, dog-brain?" asked Jamila.

Splat!

"Aieee!" Jamila shrieked, wiping the bird droppings from her face.

"It's good that you are so pretty," said Kai, "because you sure are silly. Now, let's get moving."

After about an hour, they reached a lightning tree. It was huge, with a trunk thick enough to live in, but it was charred and blackened. It had been struck by lightning and was nearly split in two.

Kai's neck and shoulders had begun to ache from the weight of the basket on her head. She sat by the tree to rest.

Jamila reached the tree a few minutes later. "Why are you stopping, Miss let's-get-moving?" asked Jamila. She didn't seem tired.

"To wait for you, Miss I-need-a-feather-for-my-hair," Kai replied.

"Well, I'm here. Let's go, then," said Jamila, taking the lead.

Kai got to her feet and put the basket back on her head. But she couldn't keep up with Jamila.

"Slowing down again?" said Jamila, looking back over her shoulder.

Kai took a deep breath and quickened her pace. *Why can't I keep up with her?*

Suddenly, Jamila stopped and waited for Kai to catch up. "Now, don't get angry," she said, "but you must change your stride. Stop bouncing up and down like a rabbit. You must take delicate steps, with shoulders back and head held high. The less you bounce, the easier it will be. Look."

As Kai watched, Jamila took a few steps, gliding gracefully. Kai tried to imitate her gait. Jamila was right. It *was* easier, but Kai didn't move as well as Jamila.

"You look like a gazelle," said Kai. "I wish I were that graceful."

"Maybe there's a thing or two I can teach you," Jamila said, laughing.

The girls refreshed themselves with water from their goatskins and started down the road once again. They joked about Bahati and other village boys, and told each other riddles and sang songs.

"What has four ears and one birthday?" asked Jamila.

"Twins," replied Kai. "Here's one. I grow on leaves, but you cannot pick me. I look like berries, but you cannot gather me. What am I?"

Jamila thought awhile. "I give up."

"Dewdrops," laughed Kai.

As the day wore on, the sun sank lower, playing hide-and-seek among the clusters of tall trees with their thick, heavy leaves fanning the sky. The forest was getting darker.

The girls walked closer together. It was getting harder to see what was on the path ahead. "Maybe we should find a place to stop for the night," said Jamila.

"Not yet," said Kai. "Granny said to walk until one hour past sunset."

"But I'm hungry and I'm tired."

"All right," said Kai. "Let's stop and have the evening meal. But we must go a little further before we make camp to sleep."

"Fine," said Jamila, sitting on a smooth patch of grass under a tree. They opened a basket and removed two pieces of dried salty fish and some melon seeds. Dessert was a small bunch of bananas from a nearby tree.

The meal tasted good. Kai could not remember a time when a simple piece of fish or a banana had tasted better.

"Let's rest a little more," said Jamila.

"Just for a few minutes," said Kai. It was always good to rest after a meal, but they had to keep moving. "We must find a more suitable place to sleep, and we'll need to gather wood to build a fire."

"Yes," said Jamila, "that's true. I should have thought of that but I didn't."

"What's wrong?" asked Kai. "You seem a little sad."

"Kai, I know that you are Granny's favorite, very smart in all things."

"That's not true. Do you notice how she glows when you are near? Even a blind woman can see your beauty."

"Maybe it would be better to be a little less pretty and a little more like you," Jamila said.

"At least you have never been teased because you can run like a boy," Kai replied. "Now I'm going to close my eyes and rest for a few minutes."

Hssss. In a flash, Kai was awake. At her feet, a forest viper slithered around her ankle. She grabbed her knife, but it was too late. She felt a quick stabbing pain in her leg.

"Oww!" she screamed.

"What is it?" shouted Jamila, drawing her knife. She saw the snake and swung the blade quickly, slashing it. It lay still for a moment, then sat up as if to strike once more. Jamila hit it again, and the snake squirmed, rolled over, and stopped moving.

"You got it," said Kai. "You got it."

"Are you all right?" asked Jamila.

"My leg, it's very hot." Kai was having trouble hearing. Everything sounded funny, as if she were underwater.

Jamila looked at the snake once again, just to be safe, and then back at her sister. Kai was sweating. Her eyes looked as if they were made of glass, and there was a bright red circle on her leg, which was beginning to swell and blacken.

Kai felt her chest grow tight. She was having trouble breathing. Her ears felt clogged. When she found the strength to look up, Kai could see the terror on Jamila's face. Then everything grew hazy. Her sister's face became the laughing face of the Oni. "This is what you get for spying on the craftsmen," he shouted. *Am I dreaming?* thought Kai. *This is terrible.*

"Oh, Kai, what can I do?" cried Jamila. But Kai didn't answer.❖

C H A P T E R   F O U R

LOST IN
THE FOREST

When Kai awoke, it was night. She opened her eyes, and they stung a little as they got used to the light of the nearby fire. She was lying on a mat on the soft moss of the forest floor, covered with a blanket, which was damp with her sweat. A shadowy figure moved closer, carrying something. As the figure drew near, Kai could see that it was Jamila, bearing wood for the fire. When Jamila saw that Kai was awake, she dropped the wood and came running over.

"How are you feeling?" Jamila asked.

"I am hot," said Kai.

"But you are shivering. You must have a fever."

"Did I fall?"

"You don't remember? You were bitten by a

snake. You slept an entire day. I worried that you would never wake up."

Kai tried to sit up. She was very weak, but she could feel her arms and legs. She breathed a sigh of relief. Before she could speak again, the world grew blurry once more, and she felt sick to her stomach. Kai fell back on the mat.

Jamila held a cup of water to her sister's lips. Kai drank it in one gulp.

She looked at her leg. It was swollen, but there was a muddy paste on the snakebite, and it was wrapped in banana leaves. "Granny Nalo's medicine pouch?" she asked.

Jamila nodded, holding up the little goatskin pouch. "I mixed the herbs with mud, like she told us."

Kai finally sat up, but she began to feel nauseated again. "Were you frightened?"

"Yes," said Jamila. "I thought you might die."

"I might have," said Kai, "if not for you."

Jamila glowed at the praise.

"Can you walk?" she asked.

Slowly, Kai got to her feet and walked in a circle. Her leg was still sore, and she felt a little sick.

"Breathe deeply," said Jamila.

Kai filled her lungs with the cool night air and the sickness passed. "We'll start out tomorrow. I think I'll be all right."

As soon as Kai woke the next morning, she knew she was better. Her head was clear, and she was full of energy. Most of all, she was hungry. After a breakfast of bananas and mangoes and a piece of fish cake, the sisters set out once again.

It was a beautiful day. Through the trees Kai and Jamila could see the blue sky and big white fluffy clouds floating by. They were happy to be on their way.

The dark woods didn't seem so strange anymore. The girls were getting used to the forest, and the forest creatures seemed to be getting used to them. Chattering monkeys swung on tree limbs above them, sometimes playfully tossing palm nuts and bananas to the forest floor. The trees were tall, over one hundred feet high.

Just then, a strong breeze came up. The palms swayed. The monkeys began to jump and scatter. Kai looked through the forest canopy to the sky. It had grown dark with heavy, gray clouds covering the sun. Mosquitoes and gnats began to buzz about them, even though it was still early in the day.

"I think it's going to rain," said Kai.

Before Jamila could reply, there was a flash of lightning and a sharp crack of thunder. The sky opened up, and a hard, driving rain began to fall. In a few moments, the girls were soaked. They moved off the path and huddled in the shelter of the trees. They were out of the rain, but the drops ran off the leaves and onto their heads and clothing.

The rain stopped as suddenly as it had started. The sounds of the animals returned to the forest, and the passion flowers seemed even more colorful after being kissed by the rain. The clouds were gone, and the sun beat down on the forest floor. The air grew so hot that steam began to rise from the wet ground.

Kai and Jamila stepped out onto the road, and sank in up to their ankles.

"Look at us," said Kai. Their legs and the hems of their wraps were caked with mud. Their sandals were completely covered.

"It's only mud," said Jamila. "It will wash off."

"You mean the beautiful Jamila doesn't mind

being mucky?" teased Kai. "Maybe I have misjudged you, Princess."

"Maybe you have, my little roadrunner."

Kai looked ahead. Granny had told them to follow the trail through the forest, but there was no sign of it. The rain had washed away the trail markers, and they could not see in which direction to go.

"Let's go this way." Kai made a decision, and they started through the soft earth. They walked a little further, but they were now more confused than ever. The ground looked like a muddy stew, and they sank in deeply with every step.

"Is this where the road was?" Jamila asked, sounding frightened.

"How would I know?" Kai replied. "Stop asking me questions."

Suddenly, the girls heard a sharp growl in the distance.

"Could that be a lion? Or a panther?" asked Jamila.

"I don't know, and I don't want to know," Kai snapped. "I thought I told you to stop asking me questions."

"Kai, I'm really afraid. What should we do?" *Growl.*

Kai looked around. She had no idea where they were. "I don't know about you, but if that cat comes any closer, I'm scaling a tree like the animals do."

Thump. A monkey tossed a palm nut at her feet, and as she looked up, Kai began to smile. "Wait a minute. That's it! If we climb a tree, we'll be able to see where we are!"

"I can't climb as well as you can," said Jamila.

"Okay, then. Just wait here." A tall, gnarled ironwood tree, with lots of vines and branches, stood only a few feet away. "Perfect," said Kai.

Growl.

"Wait for me," said Jamila. "I'm coming."

"Good. Now set your bundle down and make yourself useful," replied Kai as she climbed on her sister's shoulders, grabbed the lowest branch, and swung onto it.

Kai braced herself in the tree and held out her arm to Jamila. "You can do this," she said.

With Kai leading the way, Jamila was able to follow. The girls climbed the ironwood tree, one branch at a time.

Jamila looked down and froze. They were thirty feet from the forest floor. "Are we high enough yet?"

"Almost," replied Kai. All around them, the monkeys jabbered.

Jamila scrambled up to the next branch. "That's okay," said Kai, laughing. "Why don't you rest there? I've got an idea."

Kai climbed higher. And higher. And higher. Just above, she could see the blue sky. *One more branch and . . .*

Kai looked around. *So this is what the world looks like to the birds,* she thought. Straight ahead, the trees began to get shorter and shorter, and then a sea of green and yellow grass began. It stretched as far as the eye could see. The wind began to blow, and the grass began to swell, like waves on the water.

The sun had nearly set, so Kai could tell that the grassland was to the north, just as Granny had said. "Jamila," she shouted. "We are almost there. We are almost to Oyo!"

"Can you see the cat?" asked Jamila.

"I'll try," Kai replied. "Yes. He's miles away, sunning himself on a big rock. I think he's asleep. Nothing can stop us now. I just know it." ❖

C H A P T E R   F I V E

WARRIORS ON HORSEBACK

The savanna grass was taller than it looked from the top of the tree, rising nearly to Kai's chest. The wind was harsh and dry, but it was a welcome relief from the sticky air in the forest. Now that the girls were closer, they could see shrubs growing among the grass, and short trees. They felt grasshoppers jumping at their ankles. They heard the barks of wild dogs and saw pheasant on their short flights across the savanna.

The road that stretched out in front of them seemed to go on forever. It was just a path where the grass had been flattened by people and animals.

"I hope this leads to Oyo," said Jamila.

"It's the road, all right," said Kai. "It goes north. I saw it from the treetops."

Overhead, the birds circled. "We can make it by nightfall?" asked Jamila.

Kai nodded, although she wasn't sure. She had never seen grassland like this before, and the thought of sleeping out in the open made her

shudder. Both girls began walking faster than they had since the start of their trip.

They decided to eat while they walked. Since all they had left was peanuts and melon seeds, it didn't make sense to stop.

"Look there," Kai said, pointing ahead. They could see the gleam of a river. The sunlight on the surface danced about like little floating jewels.

The girls made their way down to the riverbank. They washed their feet and legs the best they could, and turned back to continue on the road.

"Kai?"

"Yes?"

"Why do you think they chose us?"

"I don't think it was the Oni. I think it was Granny."

"But why would Granny want us to go on such a dangerous journey?"

Kai fingered the brass figure around her neck. "She said we would find out when we got to Oyo. It can't be far."

"Thanks to you. If you hadn't thought to climb that tree, we'd still be in the forest, walking in circles," said Jamila.

Kai turned to look at her sister and smiled. She hadn't stopped to nap. She had saved her from the snake. Suddenly, Kai stopped walking and gave her sister a long, tight hug. Jamila giggled.

"I love you, my lovely sister," said Kai.

"And I love you."

Granny knew, Kai thought. *She knew that Jamila and I would grow closer on the journey.*

Kai watched the birds feed along the river, and her thoughts drifted to the future. She thought of Jamila's wedding, which was less than a year away, and of the visit from the family of her betrothed next spring. By this time next year, Jamila would be living in another compound, away from their parents, from Kai, and Bahati. "I will miss you," Kai said.

"What do you mean?" asked Jamila.

Kai was about to answer, when suddenly, a small flash of light stung Jamila's eyes. "What was that?" she asked.

"What was what?"

"Over there," said Jamila, pointing to the southeast. "There's something out there."

Kai couldn't see anything. "Maybe it was the sun playing tricks. Let's go."

They continued walking for a few minutes, then stopped and turned at the same moment.

"Now I see it," said Kai. The ground was vibrating, and there was a kind of rumbling sound. The girls could see a large cloud of dust moving in their direction. They crouched in the grass, out of sight.

"It's the sound of animals," said Kai. She had heard stories of stampedes, when a herd of wild beasts charged all at once, trampling everything in their path. "What if it's a herd of elephants? Or rhinoceros?"

The dust cloud was getting closer by the minute, and the girls could now see that it was indeed a group of galloping animals and that there were men astride their backs. As the riders approached, jackrabbits, squirrels, small antelopes, and birds scattered in all directions.

"The animals. They're . . . *horses*," Kai said in amazement.

"But they're so large," said Jamila.

The girls had never seen such large horses. The small ponies that lived in Ife could never carry a grown man very far or gallop that fast.

"They look like warriors," said Kai. "Look, they are carrying spears and swords and wearing battle vests."

"Well, I'm not waiting around to see if they are friendly," said Jamila. She stood up and began to run, dropping her bundle.

"Jamila," said Kai, "even I can't outrun a horse."

"Then I'm going to hide."

"Too late. They've seen us."

As the men rode toward them, it took all the sisters' courage to keep from running away.

"Don't let them think you are afraid," whispered Kai.

"I'm not afraid," answered Jamila, "I'm *terrified!*"

The man with the most colorful helmet and the most beautiful horse stopped in front of them. *He has to be the chief,* thought Kai.

"Who are you?" he asked, slapping his thigh.

"Kai of the Ikbani clan of Ife," she said.

The men laughed. "We are Yoruba people, like you. But you are a long way from Ife," said the chief.

"I have been traveling with my sister. We have a message from the Oni for the Alafin of Oyo."

"Is that so?"

"He gave us a royal staff with the head of Oduduwa. Jamila, give it to me," said Kai.

"I thought *you* had it," replied Jamila.

The chief snorted. "One day you will be a great teller of tales, for you have a great imagination." All the warriors laughed at this.

Suddenly, another warrior, much younger than the first, began riding around in the marsh by the river. He stopped and reached down into the tall reeds. "Perhaps she tells the truth," he said, holding something up for all to see. It was the royal staff.

"The yams are blighted in our village of Ife," said Jamila. "We need help or we will go hungry."

"Luck is with you today," said the chief. "I am Konata, leader of the Esho, the elite soldiers of the

Alafin. We will take you to Oyo." He slapped his thigh again.

Without waiting for the chief to speak further, the young man held out his arm to Kai. "Come," he said.

Kai took his arm, and he pulled her up onto the horse's back. "Don't be nervous," he said. Kai blushed, for she had never been on a horse before. "My name is Afi, of the Moremi clan. I will see that you do not fall," the warrior went on, sounding very confident.

Konata laughed and held his arm out to Jamila. In one smooth motion, the chief lifted Jamila onto his mount. "Stop shaking, young one," he said, "or you'll frighten the horse."

Konata turned his horse toward the trail and galloped off. The mighty Esho soldiers, all seventy of them, followed close behind.

Kai wrapped her arms around Afi's waist and held on tight. ❖

CHAPTER SIX

OYO

It took some time for Kai to get used to the movement of the horse. By watching the others, she learned to rise and fall with the horse's motion. She had never traveled so fast. As she watched the land speed by and felt the wind on her face, she could not stop smiling. From the mount, she could see well over the tops of the grass. It was so much fun that she almost forgot about her mission and about Jamila. She wished she had her own horse.

"Afi, why are there no horses such as this in Ife?" she asked. "The only horses there are small and weak."

"The forestland is not kind to them. There is very little food for them to eat. And there are tsetse flies, which carry a disease that can kill horses."

"Have you been to Ife?"

"No, but I have heard many stories," he replied. "It seems like a fine village. Now don't you worry about the yam blight. I am sure the Alafin will help. He will provide the food you need."

"I hope you are right," said Kai. Afi just smiled.

As they rode along, the girls saw the rocky highlands in the distance, the rolling hills of the grasslands, and the baobab trees that were scattered about here and there. Kai looked back. In the distance she could see the edge of the forest, a wall of trees between her and her clan in Ife.

One of the men rode toward them and held out two large pieces of dried meat. Another offered them water. The girls thanked the warrior and tore into the food. They'd forgotten how hungry they were.

"Look," said Afi. "Oyo."

Kai turned and saw the great city up ahead, in the shadow of a range of low, rocky hills. The town was surrounded by double walls of clay that were taller than any man or woman, about twenty feet high. Just outside was a deep ditch, and beyond that, dense woods that grew all around the town.

As they approached the main gate, Kai noticed

a beautiful, lifelike figurine dangling from a
leather cord around Afi's waist. "That's a fine
sculpture," she said.

"Thank you," replied
Afi. "My mother made
it."

"The women of
Oyo know the craft
of casting brass
sculptures?"

"Of course,"
replied Afi.

*Granny knew this,
too,* Kai thought. *She
wanted me to discover what
women can do in Oyo.*

She looked at her sister, Afi, and the chief, and
for the first time since they left Ife, she was not
afraid. She felt that something special was about
to happen.❖

A F T E R W O R D

JOURNEY TO 1440

The Yoruba people, one of the oldest African civilizations, have lived for thousands of years in an area that is now Western Nigeria. Admired throughout the world for their early achievements in economics and government, they were among the first societies in sub-Saharan Africa to develop a complex system of cities and towns. Most of all, the Yoruba are known for their arts and crafts.

According to legend, the Yoruba are descended from Oduduwa, a supreme being who came down from heaven on an iron chain and established the village of Ife. His sixteen sons then went out to form their own kingdoms. By the eleventh century, villages

Map of Africa, showing the location of Yorubaland

like Ife and Oyo had
grown into cities, with
palaces, central
courtyards, and high
walls. Even though the
Yoruba lived in separate
kingdoms, they shared
a common culture.

The entrance to a walled Yoruba village

The vast Yoruba homeland includes a variety
of geography and vegetation. There are swampy
forests along the coast and, moving north, a rain
forest, oil palm bush, high forest, woodlands, and
finally the savanna grassland. Seven rivers flow
through the territory. It is usually warm, with
temperatures rarely falling below 50 degrees; in
the summer it can rise to over 100 degrees.

Kai's village of Ife was in the south, in a
lowland forest. It was also called Ile Ife, because
Ile means "original home." Oyo was in the
extreme north, more than a hundred miles away
on the edge of the highlands. It was surrounded
by rolling savanna country and giant baobab trees.
According to legend, Oyo means "slippery place,"
and it was so named because it was the place
where the founder's horse slipped and stumbled.

In Kai's time, Ife was the center of Yoruba life

and culture, and all the kingdoms looked to its ruler and spiritual leader, the Oni, for guidance. At this time Ife was also a center for the arts, and many believe that Ife art reached its peak during this period. The rendering of the cast bronze and brass heads was very sensitive and lifelike, and these works are considered among the most beautiful

An Ife terra-cotta head

sculptures ever produced.

The artists Kai observed used a technique called the *lost wax method.* The artist first makes his or her sculpture from clay and then covers it with a layer of beeswax. The artist etches the wax so it conforms to the figure. Then he or she adds another layer of clay. When the clay is dry, the artist melts the wax and pours it out, leaving a mold with an empty space between the two layers of clay. The artist then pours hot metal into the mold; when the metal cools, the artist breaks off the clay shell, revealing a metal sculpture exactly like the one first made of clay. Since the clay mold is destroyed in the process, the artist can make only one sculpture from each, so no two figures are identical.

The principle of the lost wax method is very

simple, but the technique requires great skill. Even after Kai discovered the secret of the lost wax method, it would have taken her many years of practice and hard work to master the technique.

Although a newer city than Ife, Oyo was on the rise in Kai's time, and would soon become the most important city in Yorubaland. Since Oyo was on the edge of Yoruba territory, the people of Oyo traded with other groups from the north and eventually with traders from Europe. Oyo was also a powerful kingdom. It was known for its skilled cavalry, which imported its horses from Arabia. These horses were larger, stronger, and faster than the smaller ponies in the south. Horses were few in the south because of the tsetse fly, which can carry a disease deadly to horses.

Yoruba kings lived in great palaces and had many privileges. They wore beaded crowns, which were symbols of their authority, since solidly beaded clothing could be worn only by royalty. Most of the kings wore crowns with fringe that covered their faces. In Kai's time, no one could eat with the king. In fact, no one was allowed to see him eating or drinking. He appeared in public only once a year, at the Ogun festival at the time of the yam harvest.

The Yoruba of Kai's time were dependent on farming. They grew many things, including maize, peanuts, beans, melons, calabashes, and yams. The farmers would prepare the land and plant seeds from January through March, but there was little farm produce to eat until June, when the first corn crop could be harvested. Near the end of June, the yam festival was held, and by July or August the first yams were ready.

Nearly everyone in a Yoruba village farmed. It was not unusual for young girls like Kai and Jamila to be sent on important missions to other villages, since men could not be spared from farming. Other occupations, however, were specialized. Each technique, whether it be weaving, dyeing, woodcarving, pottery, or brass casting, was known only to a select few artists, who protected this knowledge from outsiders.

This specialization served a purpose. The people in the village learned to work together because no one group or person could produce everything for himself. When a woodcarver needed tools, he had to get them from the blacksmith. The blacksmith got his clothes from the weaver. If the weaver fell ill, she got herbal medicines from the healer.

Every Yoruba was born into a clan, and the members of the clan lived together. The eldest male member of the clan was called the Bale, "the father of the house." Parents and children lived in the same house, but to the Yoruba people, the clan was more important than the immediate family. Even though Kai and Jamila were blood sisters, they would have called every girl in their clan "older sister" or "younger sister."

A best friend was called ore ko-ri-ko-sun, or "friend-not-see-not-sleep," to signify that best friends did not go to sleep without having seen each other. In times of trouble, a Yoruba would always turn to his or her best friend. Men's friendships were often for life, but women were usually separated from their best friends when they married and moved to their husbands' clans in other compounds or villages.

Many centuries after Kai's time, many Yoruba came to the Americas, especially South America, and the Caribbean, where they made significant contributions. The Yoruba continue to prosper in their ancient homeland as well, where their art, religion, and music are an important part of Nigerian culture and the rich African heritage. ❖

DAWN C. GILL THOMAS grew up in Brooklyn, New York, the youngest of three sisters. As a child she listened to the stories her parents and relatives told about their homeland, Barbados, West Indies. The stories of her Spanish-speaking students at P.S. 9 in Brooklyn inspired Ms. Gill to write *Mira! Mira!* and *Pablito's New Feet*, while her own West Indian heritage was the inspiration for *A Bicycle from Bridgetown.*

Ms. Gill has written more than one hundred children's stories for magazines and reading series. A mother and grandmother, she lives in Barbados, West Indies, and Brooklyn, New York.

VANESSA HOLLEY was born in Portsmouth, Virginia, the second of four children. She remembers loving to draw as early as the age of three.

Ms. Holley studied commercial art and illustration at Pratt Institute in Brooklyn, New York. Her artwork combines her love of figurative drawing with her fascination of capturing the essence of the people she draws. Noted for her drawings of children, she is frequently commissioned as a portrait artist.

Juliet *Circa 1339*

Marie *Circa 1775*

Kai *Circa 1440*

Shannon *Circa 1880*

Enter a whole new world of friendships and exciting adventures!

Share the adventures of the young women of Girlhood Journeys™ with beautifully detailed dolls and fine quality books. Authentically costumed, each doll is based on the enchanting character from the pages of the fascinating book that accompanies her.

- Join our collectors club and share the fun with other girls who love Girlhood Journeys.
- Enter the special Girlhood Journeys essay contest.
- For more information call 1-800-553-4886.

Ertl Collectibles
LIMITED

Actual size of doll is 14".

GET READY TO GO ON A JOURNEY!

Join our Collectors' Club and share the fun with other girls who love Girlhood Journeys.

We've created the Girlhood Journeys Collectors' Club especially for girls like you—
bright and full of fun, and always ready to travel.

*Read about it...*in your free issue of *Girlhood Journals*, the newsletter that features interesting articles about *Girlhood Journeys* writers and artists, photos and stories from around the world, and excerpts from forthcoming books.

*Wear it...*on your hat, jacket, or backpack. You will be in fashion with a *Girlhood Journeys* pin.

*Write it down...*in your *Girlhood Journeys* Journal. You can create your own stories and characters or just jot down notes and ideas. We even give you a *Girlhood Journeys* pen!

*Hang it...*on your wall or place it on your desk. We're talking about a beautiful, signed, full-color illustration created especially for Girlhood Journeys Collectors' Club members.

Okay so how do I join? Membership is available with your purchase of a *Girlhood Journeys* doll. Simply look for the membership application form and information inside your *Girlhood Journeys* doll package.

YOU COULD WIN A *GIRLHOOD JOURNEYS* TRIP AND CHOOSE YOUR FAVORITE ADVENTURE!
Other great prizes too! See official rules below for complete details.

- Explore Kai's world on an African safari adventure.
- See the streets of Paris where Marie lived and danced on a special Paris holiday.
- Tour the castles and kingdoms of Juliet's time on a trip to London and the English countryside.

Or

- Ride the cable cars in San Francisco and visit Chinatown and Victorian sites where Shannon and her friends once played.

HOW TO ENTER: Write your own *Girlhood Journeys* adventure story about your favorite *Girlhood Journeys* doll. The story should be no longer than 500 words. Let your imagination run wild! The winner gets to choose the trip of her choice and have her story published in the *Girlhood Journals* newsletter.

OFFICIAL RULES – No Purchase Necessary

1. HOW TO ENTER: To enter the *Girlhood Journeys Writing Contest*, type or print on 8½"x 11" paper your name, address, age, daytime phone number (with area code) and your original 500 word or less essay written about an adventure taken by you and your favorite *Girlhood Journeys* doll. Mail your entry to: Girlhood Journeys Writing Contest, P.O. Box 8947, St. Louis, MO 63101. All entries must be received by December 31, 1997. The Ertl Company, Inc., is not responsible for late, lost, damaged, misdirected or postage-due mail. Illegible or incomplete entries will be disqualified. Only one entry per entrant. Entries must be original and not previously published in any medium. All entries become the property of The Ertl Company, Inc., and will not be returned. Winner must sign a release signing all rights to The Ertl Company, Inc.

2. JUDGING: The winners will be selected by an independent judging panel, whose decisions are final on all matters related to this contest, on or about January 31, 1998. Winners will be selected based on originality/creativity, writing skill, and appropriateness, in equal value. Only one prize per household or family. All prizes will be awarded.

3. NOTIFICATION: The Grand Prize winner will be notified by mail on or about February 15, 1998. Prize will be awarded in name of winner's parent or guardian who will be required to sign and return an affidavit of eligibility and liability and publicity release within 14 days of notification. Grand prize winner's travel companion must also sign a publicity/liability release and return it within the same time period. Travel companion must be 18 years or over or traveling with a parent or guardian. In the event of noncompliance within this time period, prize will be forfeited and an alternate winner will be selected. Any prize notification or prize returned to the sponsor or its agencies as undeliverable will result in disqualification and the awarding of that prize to an alternate winner. Acceptance of prize offered constitutes permission to use winner's name, biographical information and/or likeness for purposes of advertising and promotion without notice or further compensation as permitted by law.

4. ELIGIBILITY: Contest is open to residents of the United Sates who are 6-13 years of age. Employees and the immediate families of employees of The Ertl Company, Inc., its affiliates, subsidiaries, advertising and promotion agencies, and all retail licensees are ineligible. This contest is void where prohibited by law, and is subject to federal, state, and local regulations. Taxes on prizes, if any, are the responsibility of individual winners. By participating in this contest, participants agree to be bound by all Official Rules of this contest.

5. PRIZE DETAILS: Grand Prize (1): Trip for winner and one (1) guest to ONE of the following destinations: Trip Choice One • Paris, Chateaux and Countryside Holiday (9 nights); Trip Choice Two • African Safari Adventure (12 nights); Trip Choice Three • London and English Countryside (9 nights); Trip Choice Four • Victorian San Francisco (6 nights). Each trip for two (2) includes round-trip coach airfare (to/from the gateway city nearest the winner's home), double-occupancy accommodations, and a guided tour or safari. Travel must be taken by February 18, 1999. Estimated retail value of each trip for 2: $2,800.00–$9,270.00 based on destination selected and departure city. Meals, gratuities, and all other expenses not specified herein are winner's responsibility. First Prize (4): Gift set of the entire *Girlhood Journeys* book series published by Simon & Schuster. Estimated retail value: $23.95 each. Total estimated retail value of all prizes: $2,895.80–$9,365.80. Winners may not substitute or transfer prizes but sponsor reserves the right to substitute prizes with prizes of equal or greater value, if advertised prize becomes unavailable.

6. WINNERS' LIST: For a winners' list, send a self-addressed, stamped envelope by March 1, 1998 to: Girlhood Journeys Writing Contest Winners, P.O. Box 8980, St. Louis, MO 63101.